THE CONTEMPORARY
ART OF THE NOVELLA

THE CONTEMPORARY ART OF THE NOVELLA

CUSTOMER SERVICE

CUSTOMER SERVICE

SERVICE

BENOÎT

DUTEURTRE

TRANSLATED BY BRUCE BENDERSON

MELVILLEHOUSE
BROOKLYN, NEW YORK

PUBLISHED IN FRENCH AS *SERVICE CLIENTÈLE*
© EDITIONS GALLIMARD

COPYRIGHT © BENOÎT DUTEURTRE

TRANSLATION © MELVILLE HOUSE 2008

BOOK DESIGN: BLAIR AND HAYES,
BASED ON A SERIES DESIGN BY DAVID KONOPKA

MELVILLE HOUSE
145 PLYMOUTH STREET
BROOKLYN, NEW YORK 11201

WWW.MHPBOOKS.COM

ISBN: 978-1-933633-52-7

FIRST MELVILLE HOUSE PRINTING: AUGUST 2008

LIBRARY OF CONGRESS CATALOGING-IN-PUBLICATION DATA

DUTEURTRE, BENOÎT, 1960-
 [SERVICE CLIENTÈLE. ENGLISH]
 CUSTOMER SERVICE / BENOÎT DUTEURTRE ; TRANSLATED BY
BRUCE BENDERSON.
    P. CM.
 ISBN 978-1-933633-52-7
 I. BENDERSON, BRUCE. II. TITLE.
 PQ2664.U812S4713 2008
 840.9--DC22
                                    2008025483

CUSTOMER SERVICE

Last Christmas my parents gave me one of the more high-tech smartphones. From then on, wherever I was in the world, I could entertain myself with a variety of electronic games, reserve taxis, send photos, get the weather report, and have access to billions of kinds of useful information on the Internet to keep from getting lost in actually living. My parents were bled dry by the purchase of the phone, which cost a lot, at a time when I earned more money than they did. They got a little conceited kick out of doing their part for the mature and dynamic forty-something man I'd become, traveling the world over on my journalism assignments, rubbing shoulders with stars at Parisian parties. To contribute to the social standing of their darling son, they had dipped into their savings, and I'd thanked them wholeheartedly before continuing my hectic life on the information highway.

A few days later, I found a letter in my mailbox from the telecommunications company I'd been subscribed to. I'll skip the details of that genial message, signed by the "Director of Customer Service," Leslie Delmare, who thanked me for having chosen the Cogecaphone Company, and who showed no hesitation in awarding me "preferred customer" status, which offered me five thousand reward points and a free subscription to the magazine *Ring Ring*, which I now receive every month. (Why the money I spend on my cell phone should finance this four-color magazine, or foster countless promotional articles, sales offers, and travel packages is beyond me, but that's how it is.)

Hardly two months had gone by before that ill-fated day when I left my phone in a taxi. I can still see myself standing on the sidewalk at the moment the tragedy occurred, plunging my hand into an empty pocket to feel around in vain for the device and running after the car that was already disappearing into the distance. There I am, in quite a state, walking into the nearest café to dial my own number a hundred times in hopes of reaching the driver, who doesn't answer. I went home a mess. How many friends, callers, and potential employers were already trying to reach me, astonished at not being able to? It was, of course, impossible to give them any warning, since my phonebook was inside the device. Add to that my guilt over my dismal mistake. Struggling against a feeling of failure, I tried to calm down, and it was only then that the full implications of the catastrophe came into focus.

In a few days I was supposed to leave for a one-week vacation in North America. I had been counting on that telephone to keep me connected, body and soul, to my volatile intellectual endeavors with a half-dozen editors. With it, I was supposed to remain reachable by the people who guaranteed my bread and butter, and who might ask me to do another article. The whole top-notch setup had just crumbled.

I couldn't stay in this limbo, with nothing in sight. Without waiting another moment, I dashed into a phone store to replace the device. The agent was wearing a cap with the Cogecaphone logo. She listened in a friendly enough way, but by the end of our conversation, I realized I was going to have to pay four times as much for a model that was the equivalent of the old one: It seems my parents had bought a "plan" that offered benefits under certain specific conditions, none of which applied in the case of a replacement. What was more, if I wanted to keep my number, I needed a certain kind of SIM card from a series that was temporarily unavailable. If I needed to travel with a phone, it would, then, be better to buy a new subscription with a new number... However, even if I chose that approach with the same company, I'd still have to keep paying for the lost telephone's subscription for a year, as my contract stipulated. Needless to say, my reward points couldn't be transferred from one contract to another. This was the kind of highway robbery that the press, when writing about the economy, suavely refers to as *a growth in the telecommunications sector.*

When I got home, furious, I decided to get in touch with the person in charge. Hadn't Leslie Delmare said I was a "preferred customer"? That was the beginning of my long journey—comparable to *The Odyssey,* but a lot less colorful—which started on the lines of a phone tree. When I dialed the company's number I thought I heard someone pick up, and I was about to exclaim, full of helpful good humor, "Hello, good afternoon, Sir, so here's my problem. . . ."

Almost immediately, a robot voice interrupted me with its slightly pinched tones and its syllables strung together with no sense of intonation.

"This-call-will-be-billed-to-you-at-a-rate-of-one-dollar-ten-cents-per-minute. Please-touch-the-star-key-now."

I don't trust these crude machines that have been replacing humans to some extent almost everywhere. The operator's job may not have been one of the most enviable, but when it comes to service, it guarantees a form of contact less annoying than stumbling from one synthetic voice to another. Knowing, however, how to suppress my feelings of rebellion, especially when I don't have a choice, I obeyed by pressing *, which brought me to the next level.

"To-choose-one-of-our-plans-press-1. For-information-about-our-new-rates-press-2. To-speak-to-an-operator-please-stay-on-the-line."

I held for several minutes, shifting impatiently on my chair, but instead of the promised operator, the cyborg returned to offer me another choice.

"If-this-is-a-business-account-press-1. Individual-callers-please-press-2."

I pressed 2. In the same way, at every stage, just when I thought a *customer service representative* was about to come on the line, a new series of steps intervened, directing me to press one or another button, to enter my account number and even my date of birth. Then a new wait would bring me back to nowhere-land where nothing happened but a musical sequence of forty seconds, an excerpt from a Johann Sebastian Bach suite for orchestra, cut off at exactly the same subdominant chord, after which it invariably started at the beginning again, defying any form of musical logic. Inside this labyrinth, the paths seemed meticulously organized to lead me each time to a new set of multiple choices—postponing ever longer any contact with an operator, who was probably drowning in the flood of important calls.

But what disturbed me the most about this dead time was the fact that it was costing me a lot. The "customer service" number had obviously been designed for cell phones and their special system of fixed rates. The service would have been almost free if I'd called from my Cogecaphone—an impossible thing to do, since I'd lost it. Conversely, if I called from a land line (I had kept my old national telephone service), I would have to hand over the exorbitant fee of more than a dollar a minute. So, while the phone tree vomited out its instructions and Bach fragments, I was mentally seeing another meter with numbered sums spinning into place; I could hear the ringing of coins tumbling out of my bank account and gliding toward the operator's.

Tainted as my brain was by these financial concerns, I saw right through this Machiavellian scheme. On the one hand, these companies lure the public with cut-rate prices, enticing offers, publicity brochures, rock-bottom fees, and months of free service (on a poster I'd even seen the offer of a cell phone for the price of a hamburger). On the other hand, once the consumer signs up, he must obey draconian rules and pay penalties if he commits the slightest infraction. Tied down by a year-long contract at minimum, he becomes a tool of the company, whose after-sale service is reduced to almost nothing, in order to ensure a high return. For the most minor complaint, the wait time is infinite and the billing for that waiting period itself contributes to increased profit. A naïve person would have called it "not enough employees." But the real mechanism is more cynical: *waiting time had been transformed into an economic agent and source of profits.*

In the middle of the afternoon, after lots of perseverance, I reached an operator. Relieved, I began describing my problem to him right away, but he interrupted me with a resounding, "Let me introduce myself, I'm Kevin Malandain...."

By cutting me off like that (just like the automated voice had already done), he was pointing to my lack of couth for not introducing myself. Nevertheless, I sensed a tone in his voice that said he was scrupulously applying the instructions he'd been given. I even had the impression—tragic as it was—of talking to an ordinary young man, brought up to live in fear of unemployment, whose completed studies in communications hadn't led to any profession. After a glimpse of the unknown, he'd found a job at this company, where he'd been hastily taught a few business rules. In order to get a lousy salary, he had to introduce himself in a certain exact way, use a list of specific phrases, appear involved in the development of the company that was exploiting him, and consider this employment to be an opportunity.

So I took my turn introducing myself before returning to the detailed account of my problems, while reminding him that I was a "preferred customer." He, on his side, made an effort to understand me, but it was obvious that he had no power or ability to make a decision, no other solution but typing my account number on his keyboard, reading what he was seeing, then repeating to me what I'd already been told at the store—that I had to keep paying my old account for a year as well as the new one, if I wanted to travel with a cell phone. As I was beginning to get worked up (all the while swearing to him that I had nothing against him "personally"), he explained the only effective method for this type of case: Address my complaint *in writing* to the director of customer service who, by the way, never took phone calls.

I still had a little energy left when I turned on my computer and typed that cordial yet indignant letter.

To begin, I brought up the benefits they'd promised me—I attached a copy of the welcome letter signed by Leslie Delmare. I stressed all the statistics that made me an ideal consumer—in my forties, single, at the top of my profession, traveled a lot, telephoned an enormous amount regardless of the cost—so this company would do well to afford me some satisfaction. I even said I was ready to buy my new telephone at the highest price. But I insisted that they release me from my old plan (in theory, I still had eleven months to pay) and that it purely and simply be replaced by a new contract, that I was ready to sign immediately. I added a few lines concerning the issue of the rewards points and my wish to hold on to them (I'd noticed in the catalogue a fruit-and-vegetable blender that I wanted). It was quid pro quo.

A week later, just before I left for overseas, Leslie Delmare sent me a disappointing answer. His form letter, which was quite cold, didn't answer any of my questions. As specified by my contract, I had to pay off eleven more months on my old plan; and as for transferring my rewards points, well, that was impossible. I'd been hoping for a personalized solution in response to my so carefully composed letter to customer service. It appeared that none of my arguments had even been taken into account. Only the flowing signature in blue ink could testify to any particular attention. But all computers can imitate a personal signature in blue ink.

Rage rose in my gut. Fearlessly, I plunged back into the telephone labyrinth. After having pressed the star key several times, after patiently waiting at the steep per-minute rate, after several shouting matches with employees who explained, one after the other, that there was nothing they could do—and I really wanted to believe them because they all seemed to belong to the same category of illiterate students, forced to utter ready-made formulas—I relentlessly climbed the phone ladder of the company. At the slightest barrier, I'd lose patience and shout; I'd remind them that I was a *journalist* and that this affair could go very far. In order to get rid of me, an exhausted customer service representative would end up asking me to wait and pass me on to his superior. But this company underling was hardly any more accountable than the lackeys at the previous level. And I held on, talked about a *media outcry*, inched still higher up the ladder and ended up with someone in charge: an agreeable and patient enough woman who listened to a recap of my arguments. When I'd finished, I added that the simplest thing to do would be to connect me with Leslie Delmare, because now it was a matter of something personal between him and me.

Once I'd arrived at this third level in the pyramid, however, I understood that I couldn't climb any higher: The middle manager tried to dodge my request; then, seeing that I wouldn't give up, explained to me in a patient voice that Leslie Delmare, in charge of customer service, didn't exist. It was just a name invented for the signature. *The only person who could take care of my problem was imaginary.* This woman's words threw me back, mind ricocheting, to all those powerless operators who couldn't make the slightest decision but were forced just to repeat the phrases they'd been taught.

Leslie Delmare didn't exist. There was no director of customer service. Its employees couldn't make any decisions and could, at best, refer cases like mine to the legal department (if I was willing to start a long process with the help of a lawyer). There was no other possible response. Better to give up this absurd struggle and lose from the start. Suddenly changing my tone, I thanked the person I was speaking with and ended up accepting the conditions they were imposing. Because despite everything—and this was the main result of all those lost hours—I now felt a connection to this company that was becoming a habit. I had no doubt that the runaround would be just as hellish with any other. It meant I had to be more alert, avoid taking a wrong step, always remain within the strict framework of the contract I'd accepted, even if I'd accepted it by mistake, during a moment of excitement, following a promotional offer designed to make me lose my good sense.

II   As I was buying my plane ticket, the Air France employee pointed out that I could change my date of return.

A few weeks later, in a hotel room in Montreal, I naturally picked up the phone and dialed the company to do just that. This time, as I waited, the inevitable recording asked me to please be patient for a few moments. But I was prepared to wait a long time: sprawled on the bed, I watched an interesting TV documentary on the reproductive habits of crocodiles. With one ear to the receiver, I anticipated my answer, like a tourist certain of his rights. A quarter of an hour went by, then a half-hour. Because I had an appointment, I finally hung up, figuring I couldn't reach Air France because of a temporary glut of calls. I'd taken precautions: I still had two days before I had to leave.

After lunch, I called again and went back to waiting. On a continuous loop with an electronic melody in the background, a soft voice that sounded like a bar hostess promised—in French and in English—that my call would be answered "as soon as possible." However, this Monday the lines seemed just as overloaded, so I decided to put it off till the next day. Tuesday morning brought no sign of hope: the monotonous voice on the machine repeated its refrain, occasionally suggesting a special number for *business or first class* passengers. Of course, my ticket was for coach, the most economical category, and thus, logically, I received the worst treatment. This time I waited forty minutes without daring to hang up, out of fear of losing my place in the queue.

Early in the afternoon, having decided to take care of the issue no matter what it cost, I took the subway and got off not far from Air France's offices. They were no longer in their old elegant boutique office on a main avenue, but instead were lost somewhere in the middle of a high-rise. I went into the branch of *my* national company on the fifteenth floor, where customers were seated in front of several closed ticket counters and two overwhelmed receptionists. You had to take a number. Forcing myself to stay calm, I thought about the fact that there was nothing tragic about my situation, compared to those unfortunate Argentines who'd waited in front of their banks the week before, hoping to recoup a part of their savings. From one day to the next, their country fell into *ruin*: They lost everything.

This comparison brought me to my senses. Looking again at the line and the roll of numbered tickets, I figured that putting so much energy into delaying my return flight by three hours for no real reason other than my modern man's restlessness wasn't such a great idea. So I opted out of this new ordeal, went back to the elevator, and returned home on foot. Lots of people were busily making their way along rue Sainte-Catherine. I stopped in front of a store window to admire a muskrat trapper's hat, which looked comfortable and warm for winter. Entering the store, I tried it on. It made me look like a logger from the Great North. Pleased, I went to the cash register and pulled out a platinum credit card from the pocket of my anorak. Then I pasted a perky smile on my face while the salesperson waited for the purchase to be authorized.

Not everybody has a platinum card. Those who do are expected to have a fairly large bank account and a regular income. It's designed to allow businessmen to withdraw any amount they want anywhere in the world...at least, that's what my banker said. And I'd left for North America feeling quite sure of myself. Three days later, I'd been struck by doubt in New York when I tried to withdraw two hundred dollars. Refusing the transaction, three cash machines in a row suggested that I contact my bank. A temporary error? A computer malfunction? Putting away the platinum card, I'd used my traveler's checks. Then I left for Montreal without worrying about it, figuring that in this nearly French place, any unwillingness to understand on the part of New York's contraptions would be transformed into newfound trust.

And yet, this one in Quebec responded *in French* that it couldn't help me. Furious, I retried the operation several times. The salesperson was now watching me with suspicion, and I felt humiliated by the setback, as if I needed to invent an excuse: "It usually works perfectly well." However, in all objectivity, I had to admit: my platinum card was letting me down in the middle of a trip.

The next morning, keeping in mind the time change, I telephoned my bank in France, where the person in charge assured me that my account was in good standing, that she couldn't understand this malfunction, but that, unfortunately, *there was nothing she could do*, because it depended upon the "Visa International network." Seething, I figured that there must be an office for the "Visa International network" in Montreal that could resolve this kind of problem. In fact, there was a number in the yellow pages, and for a moment I thought I'd had a victory. On the telephone a pre-recorded voice invited me to choose among several numbered options: For-English-press-1. Pour-Français-faites-le-2. If-you're-a-business-press-3, etc. Without getting disheartened, I proceeded into the labyrinth and finally reached an operator. Her conclusion was without appeal: After having consulted several of her co-workers, she confessed to me that Visa International's Canadian services weren't authorized to resolve my case because they only dealt with Canadian issues. *There was nothing she could do.*

There was nothing that Leslie Delmare could do, either. No one could do a thing for me. Except for the friend who loaned me some cash, so that my vacation could come to a decent end.

After my stay in Canada, I spent a last day in New York. The evening of my departure for France, I arrived at Kennedy Airport two hours early, as required because of the current unrest. I went through the pre-boarding check, pulled my pockets inside out, opened my computer, emptied my toiletries bag, and put up with pushy questions from a fat Korean-American woman dressed in a customs outfit. Although she worked in an international airport, this woman seemed incapable of understanding that not everyone spoke English: she barked out her questions while chewing gum, and I purposely pretended not to understand a thing. But the idea of enunciating more clearly never even crossed her mind. She stared idiotically into my eyes and without the slightest effort repeated her garbled barking. To get even for my bad attitude, she made me take off my shoes to verify that they didn't contain explosives. It was midnight, but I had plenty of time. The plane was going to be at least three hours late.

I was kind of expecting this. I'd reserved a seat on a flight that was half-empty, hoping that I could stretch out and sleep. But it just so happened that a Boston-Paris flight, which was also half-empty, had just been cancelled for "technical reasons," and its passengers would be joining us that evening. The Machiavellian strategies were getting easier to read. It seemed to me that the companies had formed large airline conglomerates like Air France's SkyTeam to allow them to dump passengers from one plane into another. Tonight, for example, an unprofitable number of passengers from the half-empty Boston–Paris flight were used first to fill up a Delta flight that was half-full (Boston–New York) and then a half-full Air France flight (New York–Paris). I'd already observed the same process on a Toulouse–Paris return flight, one Saturday afternoon when all the planes were cancelled one after another for *technical reasons* (this phrase was enough to keep passengers' mouths shut). Actually, these planes were almost empty, which allowed the companies to fill to bursting a single plane, at the end of the afternoon. Of course, when he's making reservations, the consumer has a choice. Do you want to leave at 1 p.m., 3 p.m., 5 p.m.? No problem. But once the tickets have been paid for, a hidden distribution operation seems to make sure of maximum occupancy. You can therefore be almost unconditionally certain that you'll leave late and be packed in like sardines during non-peak periods.

On my red-eye flight above the Atlantic, I tried to concoct an imaginary political scenario. Suppose that a country decided to fight against inflation, against the insanity of the stock market and business encouraged by the international powers. Suppose that this revolution didn't lead to war, that neither the United States nor the European community opposed a choice endorsed by a majority of citizens (which is fairly improbable, since most people prefer international norms, but let's suppose it anyway). A new General de Gaulle would lead this plan based on the self-sufficiency of industry and agriculture. Despite attacks by an opposition party (which would call it "fascist"), it would re-establish public services and their workforce, expand schools and education, assure a balanced and stable system of economy whose controlled profits would for a long time guarantee prosperity for all—just as democratic socialism promised in the past, before the entire world seemed to become devoted to the obligatory and permanent reappraisal of that balance.

It could be the subject of a story. But how to take into account desire and frustration—the weapons of modernity? A few days earlier, I was taking the train from Montreal to New York—an archaic vestige of a train that took eleven hours to cover a little over three hundred miles, on a line with a single track. An elderly gentleman in a cap went from one car to another with a bell, serving drinks and sandwiches. The sluggish locomotive chugged along beside lakes and through the forests of the Adirondacks. A few rows behind me sat a group of Amish passengers from that Pennsylvania community that lives exactly as it did in the nineteenth century: They work their fields with horses, refuse to use telephones or electricity. Two mothers in long black dresses and scarves were keeping an eye on their children. A short distance away, the two fathers were sitting next to each other in their round peasant hats. They were about forty, but they seemed to take their role seriously. Abandoning their horses and carriages for this long trip, they'd chosen this crude train, which was a lot calmer and slower than the plane.

When I got up to go to the toilet, I took a discreet look at them. The mothers were disciplining their children with the strictness of another time; the fathers seemed lost in silent reflection, despite the tones of an electronic game, whose nervous beeps kept repeating in the car, disturbing the meditation of these peasant fundamentalists. Then suddenly, I noticed that those annoying detonations were coming directly from the two men in black hats. The peasants from the nineteenth century weren't lost in reflection; both men were bent over two idiot machines with liquid crystal screens. Obsessed, they manipulated the buttons, trying to win a few points. They seemed to be sitting a little apart, hiding from their wives so that they could take from their pockets these contemporary playthings, which their hyper-authentic life frowned upon.

I love the out-of-focus feeling of jet lag, that strange lightness that suddenly envelops familiar sights. After arriving in Paris early, I hung out all morning on the streets of the capital to study the walks, attitudes, smiles—so oddly different from those in New York. At the foot of Notre Dame, wearing my trapper's hat, I sat on a bench to eat a sandwich in the golden light of February. At the end of the day, my mind deliciously hazy with fatigue, I headed toward Montparnasse. I was meeting my cousin's son at the bar of La Coupole: he was a fifteen-year-old boy who'd been teaching me how to use the Internet. In exchange, I'd offer him press passes to film screenings. With a few lessons, I'd made rapid progress in using my PC—even if I was also aware that in the eyes of my young guru I was more like some kind of handicapped person, a man who was already old and didn't know most of the things that count today. On the other hand, his telephone call just after my arrival allowed me to tell myself that he thought I was capable of progressing: He was hell-bent on presenting me—after his classes—with a Diagnostic Doctor CD, which was supposed to clean my computer of all viruses and defects that prevented *optimal functioning.*

Since I was a bit early, I ordered a whiskey at the bar, where the staff seemed somewhat troubled by my presence. Although it had been a place for friends to meet for quite some time, ever since the renovation of the brasserie, the old "bar américain" was like a compressed airlock for tourists. They forced the customers to wait there in front of sugary cocktails before shepherding them to the restaurant's tables. But they didn't like it if a customer put down roots there. As I puffed on a cigarette, the bartender made some audible coughs. A group of businessmen visiting from Toulouse for a marketing seminar were admiring the painted pillars and Cubist chandeliers of this shrine to the 1920s—entirely demolished a few years ago. The architects had reproduced them at the exact same places, creating a very faithful replica of the old Coupole. A worthy real estate compromise was preserving picturesque Paris, on the ground floor of an office complex.

This is what I was thinking when I heard the ring of a cell phone. Several hands plunged into pockets, each man wondering if it was his. But it was my new Sagem cell phone's tinkle. Then the voice of my guru:

"Sorry, I can't come. Too much work for tomorrow. My mother will make a stink!"

I reassured the high school student that we'd see each other another day. Besides, I wasn't averse to hanging out a bit more. I ordered another whiskey. For a moment I considered trying to hook up with the young blond manager who'd smiled at me. But she stuck with the people in her seminar, and I chose to head for the door and start for home into the Parisian night.

The sidewalk led me past a series of computer supply stores, art galleries, antique shops. Several bistros in the process of being demolished would soon house ready-to-wear brands. I counted five banks. Then I started down boulevard Saint-Michel, where the lighted fruit and vegetable stands of an Arab grocer reminded me that I was in a city whose inhabitants lived, ate, drank...was this little grocery enough to feed the entire neighborhood? Had most of the residents opted for online shopping? Did they go to the giant supermarkets at the edge of the city every Saturday? Wondering, I headed north again, past the iron fences of the Luxembourg Gardens, opposite a line of Haussmann-style buildings.

When I was a child, my father once told us about a friend of his, an executive in a large American company. Though still young, this man was already worn out, in bad physical and mental health, because each year he had to guarantee profits that were higher than those of the previous year. This bizarre rule generated an atmosphere of tension, leading inevitably to depression—far different from my father's respectable position, which required him only to do his work and ensure the smooth functioning of a public institution. This story seemed strange and harsh to us, almost barbarous, like the description of a ruinous mental illness. No one could have imagined that the syndrome victimizing that friend would a few years later become the very principle of the French economy, which was supposed to "modernize" while it endured the attacks of restructuring and the imperative to increase profits.

In this transformed world, the Arab grocer almost single-handedly assured the persistence of a traditional form of living, among services and businesses with a strong appreciation in value. There was very little traffic; my steps rang out on the street, and the boulevard looked like scenery for a nineteenth-century novel into which some contemporary content had been inserted. On the corner of rue Soufflot, the student brasseries had given way to the flashing red of fast-food restaurants, which superficially imitated Parisian-style store windows. Other transformations seemed subtler: Recently the 1960s streetlamps had been replaced by authentic copies of 1860s gas streetlamps. Paris was making an effort to look like Paris, to remain a splendid city; white clouds sped above the big trees of the garden.

The door to the building in front of me opened,

between the "Connections Galore" shop and the "After Life" insurance office. I was absorbed in my thoughts about the passage of time but noticed the rotund silhouette of a priest from another age stepping out onto the sidewalk. His black cassock, tied at the waist with a canvas belt, extended almost to the ground. He was wearing socks and a pair of sandals. For a moment he stopped and studied the city with confidence. Emerging from a plastic collar, his still-young face framed by long hair displayed a real sense of assurance, a faith from the Middle Ages. Everything seemed to indicate that this priest was a traditionalist. With curiosity I studied this vestige of a world that had disappeared. He stood erect at the crossroads between digital services and hamburgers.

A young modern-looking couple had come out of the building behind him, probably leaving the same gathering. They exchanged a few words with him in front of the entrance. I walked by, listening.

The priest to the couple: "So come and visit my presbytery one of these days."

The woman to the priest: "Well, it certainly was nice of you to come. Try to be free for the school alumni evening."

"I can't get away from my scouts in the middle of a pilgrimage to Chartres."

Having passed them by several feet, I turned to see the ecclesiastic moving away, his slightly lumbering Catholic step heavy with belief in God and the Devil. As he crossed the street, he pulled up his cassock.

Mechanically he stuck his hand into his pocket and took out a small object that he held in front of him, pointing it toward the street. The headlights of a Renault Twingo blinked twice. With an innocuous gesture, the servant of the saintly Pius X had just operated his electronic key. In his black robe, he incarnated all the will to resist change, yet his modern man's chrome bodywork was practically champing at the bit as it waited for its master. And I thought: This priest wasn't a creature from another time; he was actually closer to the real-fake streetlamps.

Casually, he climbed into his car, buckled the seatbelt, turned on Radio-Notre-Dame, and took off onto boulevard Saint-Michel, lowering his window to call out to his friends, "I'll call you about that modem stuff, but believe me, you'd do much better with a cable connection . . ."

The friends disappeared into the adjacent street, but, a few seconds later, I was surprised to see the priest's car suddenly brake, with screeching tires, in front of the McDonald's sign. Instead of going directly home, the man of God got out of his vehicle and walked into the hamburger shop with his rolling gait. When I got to the window of that fast-food joint, I saw him waiting in a line that stretched from the counter. Without shyness, he said something to a bearded North African who was waiting in the other line.

I pushed open the door of the place and stood with the customers to get a better look at this new kind of missionary. The North African was wearing an untrimmed beard, in the style of Islamic fundamentalists. His closed features betrayed an irritation mixed with surprise about the advances of the priest, who was gabbing uninterruptedly, combining religious arguments with a passion for high-tech.

"I'm Christian. You're Muslim, and I respect you, because we have the same God. We can all come together with computers. I organize free Internet training classes Wednesday afternoons, would you be interested in coming?"

Far from distrusting such a proposition, the Muslim raised his beard to ask, "On PC or Mac?"

The priest knit his brow. "I know everything about PCs, but even if you're into Mac, we should be able to work it out."

He took a business card from his cassock and held it out to the man, who looked at it attentively. Then he ordered a milkshake and went back to his car, his sandals firmly slapping the asphalt, as if in the diocese of a new world.

IV   The next day, I got up early. Invigorated but broke from my week of vacation, I turned on the computer to begin work. My bank account was almost empty, and I had only three days to write an article about "forty-somethings," an assignment from a magazine with a large circulation. The work stood to bring in the equivalent of two months' rent and, more than that, renew the respect of my peers, who'd notice my incredible talent for bouncing back. Past forty, I wasn't marginalized, finished, worn out, exiled from the circle of cultural commentators. I still frequented the editorial offices like a tenacious, if aging, young man. A few weeks before, a short-lived inspiration during a meeting with a young editor-in-chief (who'd been my subordinate five years earlier) had led to my suggesting the topic. "They're forty and they refuse to grow old. CEOs in baseball caps, young dads crazy for adventure and strong sensations, they've given up on changing the world, but not on realizing their dreams."

Not so long ago, I would have snickered at such a thing, but my cynicism was beginning to seem more and more like a dead end. Besides, a large part of my generation (especially those who followed new trends in magazines) probably identified with this model: adult and teen, playing with PlayStations and buying the latest Goncourt-prize book, investing in stocks and smoking their joints. To match the zeitgeist of the magazine that was hiring me, I promised myself to approach the subject from a positive point of view; I was ready to include the idea of "progress," the picture of a world where men and women were clear-sighted, more generous and more equal, more tolerant. All I needed to do was collect a few concrete details to fill out the article and give the impression of legwork. Since it was cold, I decided to go on the Internet. I could do my research with a search engine and wouldn't have to leave home.

While the machine was connecting, I banged out a first draft of my introduction. But I'd barely finished those dozen lines when the screen froze. Nothing happened when I hit the keys, the text remained stuck at its last words, "more clear-sighted and less rebellious," as if the computer itself were revolting. The rest of the screen was covered by a smaller window with terse text that ordered, rather than asked:

ENTER YOUR PASSWORD.

A bit surprised, I searched my memory and typed *password*, the access code registered a few months earlier for my free Internet connection. The computer answered:

INCORRECT PASSWORD. TRY AGAIN.

I retyped each letter more meticulously, and got the same response. The computer stared back at me obstinately, and I soon had the impression that it was toying with my nerves, as if such things amused it sometimes. Just when I'd think everything was going well, it would ask me an incomprehensible question, subtly disrupt the page layout, put me through ordeals that I could rarely recover from on my own.

The request for a "password" usually didn't intervene except during some specific maneuver: reading my e-mail, checking my bank account . . . for these actions, I'd memorized a series of letters and numbers meant to protect me from malicious intrusions. Actually, I could hardly see who, among the millions of Internet users, could really feel a need to raid my hard drive; but my guru was adamant when it came to this subject, and he was plagued by a phobia for uncontrolled "attacks." And I had blind confidence in him, ever since the day he'd walked into my place like the Savior. At the time, I'd just bought my PC.

For twenty-four hours I'd tried in vain to use that brand-new machine. I was almost in tears before the screen when my cousin sent his son to fix things. In a few moments, this little cyber-genius had figured out what I needed to do to boot up for the first time; he always knew how to respond to the questions or terms in English: "O.K.," "Cancel," "shut down" or "timed out." From then on, I followed the dictates of this kid, so full of himself, and who, among other instructions, had saddled me with this list of passwords.

Even so, the computer had never demonstrated its ill will when connecting to the Web. Had a "bug" crept in during the steps of booting up? Perplexed, but wanting to go back to work quickly, I tried other combinations I had in my head: my birth date, my first name, my ex-fiancée's...all attempts were fruitless. With cold arrogance, the PC would answer:

INCORRECT PASSWORD. TRY AGAIN.

Rummaging in the laptop bag, I found other secret codes scribbled on scraps of paper that occasionally allowed me to access online games or to download porn photos. I typed Fuckyou, then ScrewYou&Yours. But the machine seemed patient, ready to play this little game for a long time until it got an answer that satisfied it. Combining several keystrokes at once, I attempted to close the inconvenient window and return to the text—but the computer wouldn't hear of it. On the tenth try, it got even more disagreeable and told me to "contact the system administrator." Exasperated (I hadn't known my PC was being administered by someone else), I ended up phoning my guru.

He answered from class, at the high school—which didn't seem to bother him very much. But when I finished explaining my problem to him, his voice sounded a little fed up. To him, my question seemed banal.

"All you have to do is quit the program by pressing control-alt-del..."

In the background, a teacher's voice droned on. Mustering all my self-control, I simultaneously pressed the three keys. Nothing happened. My guru thought some more.

"Try to reboot."

Despite his "expert" act, this little brat didn't understand my problem at all. If I turned off the computer to reboot, I'd lose the introduction to my article, hidden by the new window (I was in no mood to type these ten stupid lines a second time). What's more, I didn't understand this sudden request for a password. While I was insisting, he shot back his automatic response for unexplainable occurrences.

"Maybe you caught a virus. Sorry, I think the history teach' is asking me a question...if you want, we can get together around five at the web café on rue Montparnasse. I'll bring my Diagnostic Doctor disc... only if you find the right *password*!"

And he hung up on me.

After sitting exhausted in front of the screen for half an hour, I decided not to let myself be a slave to technology. I found a simpler solution for taking advantage of the coming inspiration by going down to the neighborhood stationery store and buying a 96-page school notebook (brand: Clairefontaine) as I had done in the past, to handwrite my article. Although I was used to the ease of word-processing and wasn't somebody with a fetish for pen and paper, I was prepared to put up with it for lack of anything better.

As I walked downstairs, I tried to recap the content of my article: the appearance of the new forty-somethings, connected to the fall of the Berlin Wall, the emancipation of women, an explosion in communications . . . I walked out of the building, turned left in the direction of the stationery store, but, feeling in my pockets, I realized that I'd left my money at home. Fortunately, right by me was the bank—or rather, what was left of my bank, since general management had closed half the branches and reduced the others to almost nothing. The three employees in this one had been replaced by a single "financial advisor," a kind of lackey whose job was to open accounts, collect checks, and sell services and contracts. You weren't supposed to count on him any more for withdrawing money: They'd replaced the teller's window and the teller with a cash machine that was inside the premises.

I pushed open the door, greeted the sole employee, who was behind his desk, and went to the cash machine to put in my platinum card. But when it came time to punch in the secret four-figure code, I realized that I'd completely forgotten it. Usually I touched the keys without thinking about it; but suddenly, despite an effort to concentrate, the combination merged into a fog with the PIN of my cell phone, as well as with the password for my e-mail and all the magic formulas that had passed through my head since morning. In that muddled orbit, I did seem to recognize a few groups of figures but no longer saw what they were connected to nor exactly in what order.

Knowing that I only had a right to three attempts, I tried to remember the combination mnemonically. Maybe the bank card was the street number of my building, multiplied by my mother's age. Not really sure, I did the calculation and typed the four numbers. The machine immediately spit out my card, and I concentrated harder, trying another combination, without any success. Distraught, I went back to the financial advisor and asked him what to do when you forget your bank card PIN. He peered at me helplessly from behind his desk, which was piled with catalogues describing "banking products."

"Sorry, you have to write in. There's nothing I can do!"

I gave up trying a third time. While waiting to refresh my memory, it would be better to go back home and get some money. My spirits weren't flagging yet, but there was no end to my disappointment when it came time to enter the building and I had to put in the code to the entrance door; because this combination of letters and numbers had been lost as well in the forest of encrypted combinations. Just then a neighbor came out of the building and reminded me that the code was 2003—like the year; it actually wasn't that complicated.

When I walked through the lobby, I mechanically opened my mailbox, and there lay an envelope with a transparent window that was about as tempting as a bill. I tore it open in the elevator. Judging by the first lines of this piece of mail—which came from a well-known Internet service provider—they were demanding a sum of eighty euros for two months of service. The CogecaNet Company were stressing how thrilled they were to count me among their customers, while also reminding me of how lucky I was to have the benefit of a high-speed connection. To make my status as a customer official, they were inviting me to sign a small detachable coupon and accompany it with a check, or to send in my bank card number. As a p.s., the person in charge of customer service was inviting me to take advantage of my reward points, which would then get me a clock radio.

All of it seemed extremely friendly . . . except for the fact that I'd never asked this company for a thing. I remembered perfectly their advertised offers, which included sundry bonuses (a subscription to *L'Express*, a digital encyclopedia, a trip to London for two...), but more than anything, I remembered having stubbornly refused that high-speed Internet service, a decision for which my guru had berated me for months on end.

According to him, this connection was *indispensable from now on*. Except for the fact that I didn't need it, any more than I needed loads of "indispensable" inventions. I made it a point of honor to resist him when it came to certain things. He'd constantly claim that my PC lacked power. I'd counter by saying that my word processor and e-mail were quite enough. He'd counterattack by installing new programs that overloaded the machine and that he said called for more speed, memory, and performance. I'd obstinately reject his offers despite all his arguments—the most harrowing being those he expressed in the tone of a missionary explaining to an African how a water pump works by saying, "It's going to change your life!"

So? Had I put in the order without realizing it (on one of those countless occasions when you have to choose among "yes," "no" and "cancel," without really knowing what you're doing)? Had my guru been pushy enough to sign me up against my will? Had he gone so far as to deactivate my free connection? Between the lost passwords and an inexplicable bill, this day was off to a bad beginning. My head was teeming with theories. The monster had reared up again: That racket concocted by today's businesses, under the pretext of communication; that diabolical link between the harassments of advertising and subscriptions impossible to cancel; that obligation to adapt endlessly to updates making an appliance that was perfectly functional obsolete ... but as I was rereading the letter in search of a telephone number, a small injury occurred in my brain.

From time to time I'd experienced this bizarre, unpleasant feeling, as if my mind were leaving my body and suddenly floating next to me. It isn't the out-of-focus feeling of jet lag, but a more schizophrenic sensation: I'm observing myself at the core of a cold, agonizing reality. At such a moment I'm afraid, that horrible fear of no longer being able to glue the pieces back together. Fortunately, it usually lasts only a fraction of a second, after which my being amalgamates and returns to its usual restlessness. However, I remained in suspension, paralyzed by my amazement as I read and reread at the bottom right of the letter the name of the person in charge of customer service: *Leslie Delmare.*

ᴠ   It was the same signature in blue ink. Like an invitation to begin again on the same path. Were all directors of customer service named Leslie Delmare? Did I have to face the ordeal of telephoning my complaints yet again, put up with unanswered letters and end with the exact same results as the first time: find out that Leslie Delmare No. 2 didn't exist any more than Leslie Delmare No. 1? Unless Leslie Delmare was a trademark, a technical assistance company that provided various after-sale services, including those of my telephone company and my Internet provider.

    With relief I caught sight of a logical explanation: Actually, all of these branches were subsidiaries of a more important consortium: Cogeca. For several years, the former state-subsidized company, specializing in the transport of electricity, had been demonstrating a fervent wish to modernize, trading in their old industry for something from the "new economy." It had bought out businesses all over the world and accumulated huge debts. Everywhere in our daily lives, its activities were characterized by a variety of trademarks: CogecaFinances (the stock market), Cogecaphone (telecommunications) or CogecaNet: running wild on the Internet and persecuting me this morning by demanding my money. Aside from the services they were offering, the function of these brands was to bring down Cogeca's debt, by collecting a maximum of money with a minimum of employees; and I was suddenly being asked to participate in this debt reduction process.

Faced with this simple analysis, my conscience reared its head. I wasn't going to be Cogeca's cash cow, and I wanted to know what kind of answer Leslie Delmare had for me. This time, as if I were leaving on a long voyage, I mustered all my strength and dialed the entry number to the labyrinth, whereupon the gate swung open instantaneously:

"This-call-will-be-billed-to-you-at-a-rate-of-one-dollar-ten-cents-per-minute.   Please-touch-the-star-key-now."

I pressed *.

"To-choose-one-of-our-plans-press-1. For-information-about-our-new-rates-press-2. To-speak-to-an-oper-ator-please-stay-on-the-line."

I waited for a few seconds.

"If-this-is-a-business-account-press-1. Individual-callers-please-press-2."

I pressed 2. But as I was giggling nervously, persuaded that the machine would tire out before I did, an unforeseen formula interrupted my new ascent toward Leslie Delmare.

"All-our-operators-are-currently-engaged. Please-call-again. You-may-also-consult-your-account-on-the-Internet."

These bastards were good. On the table was a letter congratulating me for a high-speed account I'd never asked for. These plans always offered me the same reward points, benefits, membership in a fraternity—when all I wanted was simply to make my computer work. I was telephoning to dispute the bill and because I couldn't even get an Internet connection. And yet, for every answer, the telephone robot invited me to check my account . . . on the Internet.

I began to boil over. I'd barely hung up the phone when it rang. I picked up the receiver. A female voice broke into a rapid spiel.

"Hi, I'm Jennifer Leduc. Are you familiar with our 'Numbers of the Heart' plan? We're offering a fifty-percent discount for three telephone numbers of your choice during off-peak hours, from March first to the fifteenth. I see that you already have the option 'Telephone Advantage,' offering a sliding scale on nationwide calls every morning—except Sunday—from eleven a.m. to one p.m. Are you satisfied with this service?"

I would have liked to torture her, while telling her about a time when billing was simple, clear, and based on only one variable. But it was obvious that this poor girl was just an ordinary prostitute, enslaved by a public company gone private that was hiring her to intrude on people's lives. I settled for hanging up on her and considered my situation once again.

On a publicity sheet attached to Leslie Delmare's letter was a photo reproduction of Arthur Rimbaud, godfather of the new publicity campaign for Cogeca. A bubble coming from the poet's mouth proclaimed, "Be absolutely modern." And under that bubble, in smaller letters, "A world of pleasure is awaiting you on the Web." In the text that followed, Cogeca held forth about its desire to help young Internet users, while favoring "daring" and "imagination." Was Leslie Delmare like that teenage poet, roaming around, "with my hands in my torn pockets"? Was he a sort of company-Rimbaud?

Regardless, I wasn't about to give up. Since he was inviting me to contact him via the Internet, I went to the Web café where I was supposed to meet my guru. There I began by writing an open letter to the "alleged Leslie Delmare," in which I summed up my doubts and my indignation. But when I wanted to go to CogecaNet's site to post my lampoon for all to see, a window told me that the site was currently "under construction" and invited me to try again in a few days.

To pass the time, I looked at close to 147,000 Web pages about Arthur Rimbaud. A lot of sites were completely devoted to him: Rimbaud.com, Arthur-Rimbaud.info, Rimbaud-boulevard, Arthur.le.Fulgur as well as Chezarthur.com. Each page suggested its own approach to the young poet: "author of the end of the nineteenth century," "mythical figure of French gay life," even "forerunner of feminism." Comparative studies brought together "Arthur Rimbaud and Leonardo DiCaprio," who had played the poet in the movies "with his plump face that is both romantic and rebellious." A site in honor of Che Guevara claimed that he had "reconciled Marx and Rimbaud." An extensive catalogue offered T-shirts, posters, postcards with the likeness of that "rebel, rascally adolescent, who is the incarnation of dissatisfied youth." In general, the sensibility was summed up by the name of another site: poète.rebelle.free.fr. In such conditions, why wouldn't Rimbaud have provided the advertising claims for a state-of-the-art company?

As an adolescent I had read his poems, whose dark, esoteric aspect had put me off slightly. I preferred the rhythmical melancholy of a Verlaine, the fantasies of an Apollinaire. However, I myself was a prototype of the neo-Rimbaud, writing countless pages of rather confused prose poetry littered with sexual or morbid imagery, which gave me the feeling of being on the side of the rebels, Rimbaud's side. I was battling for transgression from a provincial Catholic school. I was fighting for the avant-garde from the heart of a bourgeois family. I was hanging out with the local artsy set, who published limited editions of other collections of poems, in free verse, which ceaselessly imitated Rimbaud's *Illuminations*. In 1977, it was still possible to think of yourself as a Rimbaud, in the face of the antiquated routines of a French sub-prefecture. In every way, that society was an evocation of yesterday's world, with its conservative environment, its outdated religious and patriotic standards to which the winds of political protest, modern art, and free morals still seemed opposed.

Today, sitting in front of this computer screen, it was obvious that I'd won every aspect of the agenda— as if the anti-values for which I'd been a propagandist had taken things beyond my wildest dreams. Each year brings its new crop of neo-Rimbauds. Writers, filmmakers, singers, who speak to us about their daily lives, their obsessions, their illicit thoughts somewhat reminiscent of *A Season in Hell.* They love gloomy atmospheres, transgressive discourses, and linguistic research. In addition to these cultural Rimbaud types, there is an increase in another type of neo-Rimbaud, those who are more lighthearted, more charming; and there are more of them every day, with their hair blowing in the wind, their noses pierced. They are the nightclub Rimbauds, blithe Internet surfers, convinced that they're bringing new blood to society, fighting dullness and old age. They have the virtue of spontaneous speech. For every situation, they know how to offer sound bytes, as if they were on a talk show. Neo-Rimbauds have ideas about everything and an ability to listen. They wear Rimbaud T-shirts the way their forebears wore a suit and tie, they are devoted to Windows like their grandfathers were devoted to their companies, they challenge capitalism the way their grandmothers went to Mass, they demand their right to housing, leisure time, and travel, and they earn a living any way they can.

These ideas were muddling my brain. For an hour I'd been Internet surfing at the Web café. I found Arthur Rimbaud schools, high schools. On September 21, 2001, the day of an explosion in a chemical factory in Toulouse, "The only telephone line that held up was the *Rimbaud*, a protected private line that links the police to the prefecture and the government." Rimbaud prevails even beyond the planet. During some public events for a celebration of poetry, the Printemps des Poètes, his work "was put into orbit in the space rocket *Ariane*."

Catching sight of a new subject for an article, I accumulated all the documents in one folder, then sent the folder to my e-mail address. I'd retrieve it when my computer worked. But a new window appeared on the screen.

UNABLE TO SEND MESSAGE. YOU HAVE NOT INCLUDED THE ADDRESS OF YOUR CORRESPONDENT.

I typed my e-mail address a second time.

INVALID ADDRESS. PLEASE TYPE YOUR PASSWORD.

What now? Since the morning my computer had been demanding passwords. And now, this machine, *which had no idea who I was*, was also asking for an access code. Wild with rage, I successively typed my sister's birth date, the secret password for my bank card, the code for the door to my building—no result. I was about to express my indignation to the person in charge when I discovered the disheveled head of a teenager bending over me, following the process with interest. My guru had just come in with his Diagnostic Doctor CD. And he was already taking charge of things.

"Try pressing alt-shift-tab or alt-shift to go to the preceding window."

I gave him an overwhelmed look. Bending toward the screen, he proceeded to do the operation himself, before concluding, "It isn't working! What a shitty system. I don't know if you'll be able to save your data. O.K., let's go to your place to find out what's happening."

With "hands in pockets," as well as a rather glum expression, my little Rimbaud headed for the door, while I gathered my things, after dragging the results of my research into the digital waste bin.

VI   Several times, my guru announced that he'd found the solution. Then, as usual, after fidgeting in front of the screen for hours, he concluded that it was better to reinstall the operating system. He backed up the data, inserted the installation discs. Since I had to go to a dinner, he told me that he'd finish by himself and that everything would be working when I got back.

The following morning, the computer still refused to log on to the Internet. Every time I tried, it responded by demanding that mysterious password—whereas there was a letter on my desk requiring payment for a high-speed connection that I'd never asked for. My telephone attempts were bumped one after the other to the telephone robot, then on to helpless "customer service representatives," out of their depth when it came to the singularity of my case. My guru stopped answering my telephone calls, and I once again suspected him of having underhandedly signed me up, in exchange for certain benefits. To get out of this, I now saw only one solution: Go on my own to the commercial offices of Cogeca, where I hoped to find someone to listen to me.

It was nine in the morning the day I walked out of the subway at the intersection of the Grands Boulevards. In front of me rose a façade covered with flashing advertisements. Giant screens projected the color image of untouched, virgin nature (forests, snow, waterfalls . . .) announcing the launch of a new portal, *Cogeca.net*. The building still looked Parisian, with its balconies and sandblasted white stone. But inside this Belle Epoque carcass, the entire interior had been demolished and renovated in the style of a marble palace for an Arab emir (an exterior from the period, a renovated interior: the opposite of La Coupole). A battalion of girls was stationed at the reception counter according to methods you'd expect from their company: Cogeca caps pulled down across their brows, long locks of bleached hair tumbling to their bosoms. They proved incapable of answering any questions except with three or four formulaic responses, one of which applied to my request.

"Oh no, this is the sales department. For complaints about your subscription you have to go to the other side of the building."

"But, actually, I never signed up!"

"It's the same. Go out, turn left and you'll see a sign that says 'customer service.'"

Reserving my fury for those in charge, I walked around the building and into a dark alleyway where I finally found the department responsible for receiving customer complaints. I pushed open the glass door. A gust of air blew into a poorly heated room with yellowish walls, illuminated by tubes of neon.

It was the lair of the lost, the second-class waiting room into which were crammed those last-resort customers who by some glitch had escaped the programmed logic of consumption. After having tried to exploit the miracles of technology; after having failed in the confrontation with their cell phone or hard drive, about twenty of the displaced were waiting for someone to agree to investigate their fate. The luckiest were squeezed onto makeshift couches; the others were pacing in nervous circles, uttering monologues full of hate; several had come with their computers, to put them at the mercy of the goodwill of technical assistance; the most optimistic were dreaming of a *repair*; they didn't know that for quite some time, a tune-up had become more expensive than replacing the device entirely—due to a lack of employees and in order to support the economic vigor of the market.

Seated behind the only counter, a young man, also tricked out in a Cogeca cap, was supposed to deal with all requests—which seemed impossible and only emphasized the pathetic status of those customers who were insistent. After flunking their entry onto the Web, it was time to enter into penance.

For the lost who ended up at customer service—after letters sent in vain, hours of trying telephone help, frustrated hopes of connecting—the rule was to take a ticket and wait for your number to be called. Despite his twenty years, the employee was visibly outmatched by the accumulation of customers. Nevertheless he remained cordial and attentive to each, as if he were fulfilling some humanitarian mission. He'd post the numbers on a lighted screen, then greet each complainant with a steadfast look on his pimply face. Then he'd have a choice among several answers that rarely matched the questions. No doubt during a brief training period he'd learned these summary phrases from a kind of directory that he kept on his desk for reference:

1. *The customer would like to cancel his subscription. You register his cancellation. He will, however, have to keep paying for the entire period of the first twelve months . . .*

At this point, the customer becomes indignant for the first time. But the crisis counselor followed this procedure:

2. *The customer wants technical assistance. The best way for him to obtain it is to use his computer to go to the webpage www.coglomo.net.*

This is when the customer typically begins to act devastated by the fact that he has already explained ten times that he can't consult the site because his computer doesn't work—after all, that's the reason he's there. So the young man lets fly the final blow:

3. *The customer establishes that the malfunction is irreparable. He must therefore send a written complaint to the Director of Customer Service.*

Given the structure of the company, which mandated selling as much as possible with a minimum of after-support, this young man represented the end of a funnel emptying into nowhere. To prepare for that drop, his job was that of the psychologist and consisted of putting up with the furor caused by customers who, at any rate, claimed not to blame him personally. After a brief silence, when all seemed lost, he'd finally suggest registering a *response-guaranteed complaint.* In other words, filling out a digital form, which was then transmitted to the technical-support services of the conglomerate, which guaranteed his receiving a repair estimate within ten days. For this estimate, the customer's account would be charged an extra one-time fee of 50 euros. At this stage, the recalcitrant consumer usually gave up and accepted paying. But even in this case, the story wasn't over because, one out of every two times, the server was overloaded and it was necessary to wait to fill out the online form for the response-guaranteed complaint. The crisis counselor would take advantage of this delay to deal with another case while the previous applicant waited for the network to become available. Behind the complaint desk hung a big picture of Arthur Rimbaud. I recognized the promotional image from my bill, which included the slogan:

The cold wind was blowing in under the door. Attached to the wall was a vending machine where you could buy drinks to restore your strength. I put in a coin, pressed the button marked ESPRESSO-SUGAR, then watched the steaming drink pouring into a plastic cup. A few sniveling sobs emerged from a girl seated on a couch. The employee, who'd just finished with a customer, came toward her saying, "Here we go, I got my connection back. Sorry for the wait, but we'll get it, finally."

An old man with a mustache said in a loud, indignant voice, "This is outrageous ... treating people like this! At the beginning, everything's polite. But the minute we have the slightest problem, we become less than nothing!"

It was going to be a long day. Spread out on a table were several issues of a trade magazine showing photos of the CEO of the company in his shirt-sleeves, posing proudly with his hand on a computer screen shining with the new Cogeca.net portal and its news features, weather, search engine. In imagery, this new world functioned perfectly. Where I was, on the other hand, the scum of humanity stagnated, were humiliated, tried to understand, to get rudimentary answers, some hope of reimbursement. A minority of them began to rebel as they discovered that their requests were leading nowhere; but their revolt produced no response.

In this dreary office where a powerless employee courageously struggled, the company seemed like a completely consolidated machine, where no one could do anything for anyone. And behind this permanent state of defeat, I saw a new situation coming into focus.

Until the fall of the Berlin Wall, capitalism had opposed with its efficiency the cumbersome bureaucracy of communism: the logic of the market versus that of long waiting lines. And yet, since the widespread victory of capitalism—focused only on relentless competition, the continual growth of profit, a nonstop reduction of costs and personnel, a fanaticism for mergers—the consumer was becoming *obligated*. While an onslaught of advertising painted in glowing colors infinite pleasures at cut-rate prices, real access to this luxury resembled a more and more perilous ordeal. Supermarket checkouts like freeway toll stations, airport concourses with formerly-public-but-now-private ticket counters where you had to wait your turn to get information, wait your turn to pay, wait your turn to pick up the merchandise, leave very late on overly packed flights, navigate miles of traffic jams at a snail's pace. And if you had the bad luck of having a problem that escaped set categories and fell through the cracks, this was the start of a much longer cycle of fruitless complaints to employees who were themselves out of their depth due to the blind logic of the organization.

In this way, a rise in productivity, a reduction in the workforce and the insanity of production were leading to a *reintroduction of communism's waiting lines in capitalist countries*; unless you belong to a well-to-do *nomenklatura* who could pay through the roof, delegate the tiresome steps, buy *business class* or get their complaints to the top of the pyramid. Big Business had replaced the Party in its method of disseminating unreal agitprop ("Buy more. Travel more. Take advantage of our terms"), while treating its customers like herds of cattle forced to adapt to the profit margins of shareholders.

However, a tiny miracle occurred three quarters of an hour later, when several numbers flashed quickly in succession, most likely because the customers to whom they referred had decided to give up and go home. With a rapidity I hadn't hoped for, the illuminated digits of my number appeared and I went up to the customer advisor, naïvely thinking that I could get an answer to my questions, despite the scenarios I'd just witnessed.

As I gazed at him full of hope, the young man turned his Cogeca cap and face full of acne toward me with a smile and assured me of his desire to find a solution. To avoid all unnecessary explanation, I handed him a copy of Leslie Delmare's letter demanding my eighty euros. He looked it over quickly, entered some data in his computer and suddenly raised his eyes with a certain respect to remark, "You were a *preferred customer* . . ."

I thought he was making fun of me. But for no reason at all (since until this moment that designation hadn't won me the slightest advantage), customer service exhibited a sudden efficiency and flexibility, and soon produced the solutions I'd been dreaming of since the first day. The advisor whispered, "We were kind of expecting your visit."

I expressed my surprise. "I tried to get hold of you by phone a hundred times, without any result!"

"I'm terribly sorry for such an unfortunate malfunction!"

I shrugged understandingly.

"Even so, this fake name for a customer service manager who doesn't exist—what kind of rubbish is that?"

I insisted on demonstrating that I knew everything about their little game. But his answer caught me off-guard.

"If you'll be kind enough to follow me, I'm sure Leslie Delmare will see you."

What had he said? The crisis counselor stood up. Abandoning the other customers, he gestured to me to follow him to the elevator at the end of the hallway. He pulled open the metallic door and pressed the button for the fifth floor. Inside the elevator he observed me timidly and spoke in an embarrassed tone. When we got to the fifth floor, the elevator opened on a carpeted lobby like the kind seen in the offices of management. Except that there were workers going back and forth in the hallway dragging cables and jackhammers. A man wearing a tie was explaining in a loud voice, "Knock down all those walls. We're going to install computers there."

My guide led me to the end of the hallway, to the only door that seemed protected from this construction work. An engraved plaque read:

LESLIE DELMARE
CUSTOMER MANAGEMENT

He knocked and gestured for me to enter.

Her appeal was obvious to me immediately—her blond hair trimmed to the level of her chin, her clear skin with hardly any makeup, her determined mouth and bright eyes, a hint of bosom below the neckline of her collar. Not for one second, in the hypotheses I'd formed about the person in charge of customer service, had I thought of a *woman*. Until that moment, Leslie Delmare's existence had seemed like a hoax to me. Now there *she* was in front of me, seated behind her desk, gazing at me with interest. It was more than obvious that my prejudices—aggravated by hours of steps leading nowhere—had been exaggerated. The director of customer service didn't look like a trendy, arrogant, flippant manager who was turned on by modern technology and negligent toward her customers. To me she seemed like a reliable woman who was attentive to practical problems, and she began with a mea culpa.

"Very sorry for this problem and the hurried answers to your calls and letters. Things started out on the wrong foot between us when you lost your cell phone; you should have been able to keep your reward points."

Her voice had the resonance of a cello, subtly inflecting from the low to medium registers. I was examining her very chic black sweater; I would have liked to take her for a drink at an outdoor café—even if I did sense something impersonal in her attitude, a warmth that was wholly professional. Still young (just forty), full of composure and authority, she gave the impression of having accomplished an intense amount of work since morning, but still not wanting to shirk any of her responsibilities.

"We're going to offer you a bonus of twenty thousand extra gift points."

A feeling of well-being invaded my body. It seemed as if, for the first time, my right to be thought of as a victim had been recognized. I hadn't fought in vain. I was going to thank Leslie when she suddenly knit her brow and added—in a sharper tone and with an authoritarian voice:

"But I can't agree concerning the high-speed connection. So, eighty euros a month is a problem for a bachelor your age? Have you given up all your ambition?"

I had explained to my guru a hundred times why

I didn't want a high-speed connection, but Leslie Delmare's tone was more intimidating. As she spoke, she was tapping away on the keyboard of her computer, reviewing my file and getting hopping mad.

"I also don't appreciate your remarks about the way today's companies are organized, your tendency to manufacture theories without really knowing us. Do you believe that we play with employees, do mergers for the fun of it? What do you really know?"

She seemed to be reading my mind. Had I said too much on the phone? Leslie Delmare turned away from her screen once again and looked at me impassively. She pressed a button, and I heard a recording of my own voice, explaining to a customer advisor, "Hello, I'm calling you because I got a bill this morning for eighty euros for a connection that I never ordered . . ."

This was followed by an obsessive enumeration of my difficulties. The operator was listening to me patiently. My explanations were endless. From time to time, I lost my temper, all the while making it clear that I had nothing against the operator "personally." The energy I was expending on getting to the bottom of this miserable tangle seemed perfectly ridiculous. As she stared at me, Leslie Delmare reminded me of my high school biology teacher—a forbidding German who used to terrorize us. She stopped the recording and continued calmly, "Seventeen hours on the telephone while the servers are overloaded. You seem to be firmly convinced that our company is evil, and you have a need to prove it to yourself . . . even if it means spending your days and nights calling us up like some nutcase!"

She paused for a moment and then asked, "Don't you think it would be more reasonable for you to do your investigations, your work, a bit more conscientiously?"

She also reminded me of that female police commissioner on a TV series that I sometimes watched on Wednesdays. I had the vague sense that she had my best interests at heart, and that was the reason why she wouldn't hesitate to notify my employers that I was working on the Internet when I claimed to be doing fieldwork. She'd put her finger on my worst fault.

"It's easy to comment on life without leaving the house! You create your little picture of the world, of capitalist conspiracies. You think you're being persecuted by machines because you don't know how to use them. But keep in mind that nobody says you have to buy them."

The explosion of a jackhammer in the hallway accompanied her exposition, causing her to raise her voice.

"Obviously, it never crossed your mind that if you're able to take advantage of our products at such attractive prices, it's because of the economies we've put in place in our departments. Our operators are in Ireland, where taxes are lower. We have software programs that answer the mail. And you're the one who's getting the benefit of it through constant discounts and prizes, you're the one who gets promotional offers every day, but you're also the one who spends your time complaining to us."

It was clear to me that the best way to deal with Leslie was to be honest, and I would have liked to prove to her that I meant well. As that thought was going through my mind, she stopped sounding coolly vindictive and returned to her cello-like tone. Accompanied by a smile, her eyes pierced mine.

"I'm not forgetting, however, that you're a preferred customer. Do you have some time today?"

Her proposition caught me by surprise. I was pretty sure that I had to meet somebody for lunch, but she insisted.

"Wouldn't it be good to take a look at reality a little closer up?"

"Yes, yes, of course . . . "

"Then follow me!"

When Leslie stood up, I got a look at her shapely, slender legs. She put on a leather jacket, moved toward the door, and gestured me to follow her through the rubble to the elevator. There was something sexy about her resolve, but I sensed that it would be difficult to steer her in that direction. In the elevator, she peered at me with her faraway eyes and showed her savvy about the human species by remarking, "You don't look your age! What's your secret?"

No, I didn't have any explanation—aside from swimming once a week and the two whiskies I drank every evening. I recommended that Leslie read my next article in that magazine with a large circulation: "They're Forty and They Refuse to Grow Old." Alternating between affection and sternness, she cut me off.

"Still, that shirt, those jeans, you should stop dressing like a teenager! You're too old! Do you have any children?"

I followed Leslie Delmare into the maze of an underground parking garage where she headed without hesitation for section G8. Her small shoes clicked rapidly over the greasy asphalt. She invited me to climb into her Citroën Picasso, and a few moments later the vehicle emerged from the Cogeca building and headed for the southern beltway. Driven along against my will, I asked timidly, "Could you tell me where we're going?"

"We're going to verify that the interests of our shareholders are the interests of everyone."

A half-hour later, Leslie Delmare pulled her vehicle into the parking lot of Orly Airport. We hadn't spoken during the rest of the ride. To provide some atmosphere, the director of customer service had tuned the radio to a nonstop news station. The news flashes followed one after another at a frantic pace due to the fact that a mass grave with fifty bodies had been discovered that same morning in the basement of a house in the suburbs—the home of a teacher who was apparently a murderous pedophile.

Leslie's restless step led me to Terminal West, and I walked behind her like a child. "Where are we going? How far is it?" She kept going, without answering.

Did she want to show me her company's public works? A village resort by the sea? I didn't understand why my complaints mattered this much to her. Obviously, her motivation was flattering, probably connected to my being a journalist, but maybe I was dealing with a manic-depressive. My complaints had pushed her over the edge. She wanted to make me see; she believed I was more powerful than I was. A free cell phone or an unlimited Internet connection with some reward points would have been enough to make me stop harassing Cogeca.

Leslie Delmare's amazing power began to become apparent when I saw the gigantic check-in line for several overbooked flights. After plowing directly toward the VIP counter, the young woman took two boarding cards out of her jacket and got me through in the blink of an eye. A half-hour later, we were sitting next to each other in a small plane with fifty seats that, according to information from the captain, linked Paris with a first-rate ski resort in the Tarentaise.

During the flight, Leslie got more interested in me. Holding a glass of Perrier, she held forth strangely about my good qualities, but also about certain of my personality traits that were more questionable.

"You've always survived on undependable work, but you keep on struggling. At forty you're hoping to get out of it; great, I admire your professional ambition! But you really should examine your tendency to grumble about everything, to find the world unbearable."

One aspect of my character seemed particularly

irritating to her. "You have to stop generalizing. Just because you forgot your password doesn't mean you're the victim of a conspiracy! Just because our company made an unfortunate mistake doesn't mean we're living in a rotten society!"

Obviously, I agreed with her.

"Look at the progress science has made, and medicine, increasing the life span! Yes, Granddad's social democracy was reassuring in some ways, but there weren't nearly as many things to choose from in stores, except for those who were the richest. Look at all the brands we can buy today at reasonable prices! Look at all the books, the hours of music and film you have access to! Doesn't that deserve some effort?"

Leslie was right, but I had my point. I tried to argue.

"Sure, but this obsessive growth in profit is going to destroy the world. There has to be an end to downsizing employees, inflating sales, forcing growth at any price, threatening the equilibrium of the planet..."

"Don't you think that maybe we've thought about those issues?"

For a moment she froze, her eyes plunging into mine with a certain melancholy. We were flying across a sea of clouds. I thought I saw a faint tear misting Leslie's right eye, and her voice broke as she asked, "You want me to be frank with you?"

She stifled a sob and then got a grip on herself and repeated in a more violent tone, "You want me to be frank with you! Well, there are days when I've had it, when I don't feel so grateful! I'm all alone, getting through a job where I have to work like a dog, my phone-tree system deals with ten thousand calls a day, my computers get a thousand e-mails a day. All that to listen to the anxieties of a preferred customer!"

She wiped her eyes on the back of her hand and abruptly turned away.

The airplane landed at the foot of the trails, under the sunny peaks of the Vanoise. As we descended the ladder-stairs of the plane, Leslie Delmare slipped on a pair of mirrored Ray-Bans that re-established a cordial distance. Then she took me to a store that rented skis and boots and ordered a complete set of equipment for me. She suggested I put the ski suit over my clothes, since we had just enough time for a spin on the trails. An employee asked me what kind of skis I preferred, and then adjusted the fastenings. As for Leslie, she chose a multicolored snowboard. Just before leaving, she instructed, "Put everything on the Cogeca account."

As we approached the ski lift, once again I was witness to the extensive world of connections of this woman. While a large crowd waited, without any hesitation Leslie Delmare went right past all of them to the line reserved for ski lessons, without provoking the slightest objection. The resort employee came to shake her hand. Pointing at the herd of skiers, Leslie whispered in my ear, "Look at the badges on their chests. Half these people were invited by Cogeca. Our Ski Weekend, which we offer to customers who have fifty thousand or more reward points. And we also provided redeployment vacations for our employees: for each company worker who opts to leave voluntarily and create his or her own enterprise!"

A lot of skiers, in fact, were wearing the Arthur Rimbaud badge under their hoods and pompoms, which identified them as belonging to the communications conglomerate. With one foot on her snowboard, Leslie kept to the side, waiting for the arrival of the ski lift. She hopped nimbly onto the chair and settled next to me. We rose through the sharp air among the torrents, above the snow-laden forests. Turning her steely Ray-Bans in my direction, she asked again, "Frankly, do these people seem unhappy to you?"

Leslie took a tube of sun block from her pocket. She handed it to me and advised me to put a lot on.

A few minutes later, we were gliding side by side among the great rocks of the combe of Saulire. The snow was perfect: a compact, rather slippery under-layer, over which stretched an expanse of powder. Getting her breath back, Leslie confessed to me that she had turned to snowboarding with great pleasure; then she executed a few hairpins in the snow.

The sun was warming. My new friend pointed toward a restaurant with a sunny terrace, and I glided behind her in an exhilarating schuss. The air lashed my face and questions rushed through my happy head: Why go around moaning all the time instead of taking advantage of this world of fantastic possibilities? I remembered the pathetic ski trails of the past, the lace-up boots and the wooden skis. Was there not something powerful, accelerated, and lyrical about modernity, as epitomized by this vast terrain of ski slopes?

Near the restaurant, vacationers were taking off their skis and telephoning each other to meet up for lunch. My companion stepped off her snowboard and invited me to follow her to the terrace. A lot of customers were waiting patiently for tables. Ordinary rules didn't apply to Leslie Delmare in this place, either; the maître d' rushed to take us to a reserved table in the sun. People stood up with big smiles on their faces to shake the young woman's hand. In the intense reflections, Leslie's skin took on its full luster, and I was proud of being seen with her. The maître d' came back to us with two glasses of champagne. The director of customer service seated herself comfortably, and for the first time that day, she seemed granted a moment of repose. Inviting me to do the same, her head turned toward the sun, and she declared, "Then take advantage of life..."

In that overly confident statement loomed a hint of anguish. It was as if she were saying to me, "Take advantage of life while there's still time!"

But she adjusted the phrase by saying, "Take advantage of life with Cogeca!"

With those words, the well-being I'd been experiencing for the last hour was replaced by a feeling of unease. Anxiously turning my head from one side to the other, I saw around me all the guests of the company, with their Rimbaud badges attached to their chests. That was when I noticed at a nearby table an imposing figure dressed in black, speaking spiritedly to a group of North Africans. He'd pushed up onto his forehead the small aviator glasses that were protecting his eyes from the sun; his cheeks were a vivid red and I immediately recognized the plumpness and the cassock of the priest I'd seen the other day on boulevard Saint-Michel. Seated at a table with a gang of lowlifes wearing heavy gold chains and hats pulled down to their eyebrows, the priest seemed totally at ease, the way you can be when you're with customers of Cogeca.

"Have you tried the new version of *Dark Age of Camelot*? It's a gas, as long as your video graphics card is at least one twenty-eight mega."

Muffled in their name-brand anoraks, the hoods expressed their approval with a few grunts. I was staring at them incredulously when someone else came over to our table and shoved me aside so that he could sit down next to Leslie Delmare. Looking up, I recognized the tousled head of my young guru, who said to my companion, "Shit, I did the coolest skiing this morning, skied all the way down to five thousand feet. There's all kinds of hook-ups to the other trails!"

Far from amazing me, the fact that he was there was a kind of proof. This little toad had been manipulating me from the beginning. He looked at me without any real surprise and said with irony, "You mean you know how to ski?"

I felt a fit of hatred rising within me, which I was going to tell Leslie about. But she didn't let me speak.

"I think you're mistaken. This boy isn't paid a cent by Cogeca. We let him have some software, invite him to ski from time to time, but he's not responsible for your problems. All he's done is make you modernize your equipment."

My guru couldn't have cared less. Slumped on his chair, he was staring up at the sky while jiggling the ice in a glass of Coke. Then, in a vision that was as philosophical as it was mystical, the two of them formed a whole for me that was close to perfection, linking youth and adulthood, masculine and feminine. Both had a taste for and mastery of modernity, a sense of the practical, and a critical sense, the desire to progress toward a better world; they formed a noble, complex entity that even someone with my cantankerous vision of the world could see. Maybe it was time for me to think about all that....

I turned my face to the sun. After the strawberry tart and coffee, I was beginning to accept my new situation when Leslie Delmare suddenly stood up and told me we were going back to the airport, because we absolutely had to be back in Paris by five.

During the return trip, the director of customer service took a state-of-the-art mini-computer out of her bag. She analyzed some growth charts, some diagrams, some color pie-charts that were proof of Cogeca's excellent financial health. She explained to me that personnel had been downsized by 70 percent in ten years and that they were hoping to reach 85 percent by next year. Obviously, the ideal would be to eliminate personnel totally and to perfect a system in which the customers did everything themselves from a computer terminal: from buying spare parts made in Third World countries to assembly and repair—interacting only with computers. They were getting close to such a thing, but the theoretical threshold of 100 percent seemed impossible to attain. Nevertheless, she asked me to read several surveys that bore witness to a high level of customer satisfaction. She claimed that even the inhabitants of the Third World, by using the Internet, were soon going to attain all the information they needed for development. She turned to face me and vowed that, in her opinion, life had a tendency to get better, though too slowly. She was working for it as best she could, with much energy and in great isolation. She needed the help of everyone!

When we got back to Orly West, without really understanding what had happened to me, I was about to go home on my own, but Leslie Delmare insisted.

"I'll drop you off, it's not that much out of my way."

The car threaded through traffic jams. On the channel with nonstop news, a commentator was explaining that this morning's scoop was inaccurate: The mass grave dated to the Middle Ages, but the owner of the house had already committed suicide. A journalist announced that France had risen two points in the monthly report on quality of life. A feminine voice was speaking to me.

"I need a guy like you."

Who was this Leslie Delmare? She went from

coldness to tears, and now to trust. I would have wanted to touch her, take her hand to feel that she really existed, but I didn't dare. The Picasso turned into my street and then slowed down. Leslie looked into my eyes once again.

"You've got to get out of this perpetual doubt!"

Maybe she really was coming on to me. She fell back into her cello voice.

"It's time to pay up!"

Was this some lewd innuendo? I tried to make a joke of it.

"Do you really want me to?"

Her answer was very prosaic. "Eighty euros. I don't even get why you're hesitating."

There was actually something ridiculous about that sum. Leslie was making it a question of principle. She was insistent.

"Do you have your bank card number?"

Then, to overcome any remaining resistance:

"Your connection will be activated tomorrow."

An excitement took hold of me, like a transposed version of sexual relations. Wanting to satisfy it, I felt around in my pocket and took out my platinum card.

"Are we going to see each other again?"

Once more she smiled.

"When I think that as recently as yesterday you doubted my existence!"

"It was your employees who told me that."

"They can't know everything."

Leslie had taken her mini-computer out of her bag.

Scrupulously she typed the numbers I was reading out to her, including the expiration date. When I'd finished, she seemed relieved and added, "I think we're going to do good things together. As a start, let me give you our new gift catalogue."

She got a leaflet out of the glove compartment and handed it to me, then asked unimaginatively enough, "Shall we kiss each other on the cheek?"

Who did I have next to me? The icy vamp who'd been fascinating me since morning, or a woman who sold vacuum cleaners? Leslie offered me her right cheek, then her left. Once I'd kissed them, I opened the door and climbed out onto the sidewalk.

When I got to the building, I turned around. Leslie had put her mirror sunglasses back on and was staring at me. For one last time, I waved at the director of customer service.

When it came time to punch in the code, I remembered perfectly that it was 2003—like the year. That was when I discovered that the system had changed during my absence. In place of the old metallic panel with nine keys, they'd inserted a new, more sophisticated machine during the day, with a camera lens for identifying visitors. Next to the camera was a numerical keyboard on which to enter the data, just by grazing it with your fingers. The digital screen showed:

PLEASE ENTER YOUR PERSONAL ACCESS CODE.

A cold sweat formed on my forehead, but I regained my

breath. Since I hadn't been warned, it was certainly still the same code. I typed the four figures meticulously. The screen displayed:

INCORRECT PERSONAL ACCESS CODE. TRY AGAIN.

I typed the entrance code a second time, but the machine insisted:

SECOND INCORRECT ATTEMPT. VISITOR UNKNOWN.
TO OBTAIN AUTHORIZATION, PLEASE CONTACT YOUR
BUILDING MANAGEMENT.

The street hadn't changed since this morning. All around me, people passed by, rushed from one place to another, went into stores and walked out of houses. In their heads they had a number of passwords with which I was currently unequipped. They followed procedures that I hadn't known how to respect. They didn't bother their directors of customer service all the time . . . turning around again, I saw Leslie Delmare, who was still sitting in her car, her eyes hidden behind her dark glasses. She was watching me with an impassive smile, as if she'd been waiting for this moment. I bolted toward her, but she quickly raised her window while saying, "Sorry, there's nothing I can do."

Then, as if she'd lost enough time, she gunned the accelerator, passed a bus full of tourists, and disappeared around the corner. On a billboard opposite my building, an advertisement showing the face of a disheveled

Arthur Rimbaud proclaimed Cogeca's slogan:
ENTER A WORLD THAT IS ABSOLUTELY MODERN,
A WORLD WHERE THE FUTURE IS NOW

I looked anxiously at the new intercom. For the time being, it was just a matter of getting into my own home.

TITLES IN THE COMPANION SERIES
THE ART OF THE NOVELLA

OTHER TITLES IN
THE CONTEMPORARY ART OF THE NOVELLA SERIES

THE CONTEMPORARY ART OF THE NOVELLA